JACK RUSSELL:
Dog Detective

Inspector
Jacques

JACK RUSSELL: Dog Detective

JACK RUSSELL:
Dog Detective

Inspector
Jacques

DARREL & SALLY ODGERS

Kane Miller
A DIVISION OF EDC PUBLISHING

First American Edition 2010
by Kane Miller, A Division of EDC Publishing

First published by Scholastic Australia Pty Limited in 2009
This edition published under license from Scholastic Australia Pty Limited.

For information contact:
Kane Miller, A Division of EDC Publishing
P.O. Box 470663
Tulsa,OK 74147-0663
www.kanemiller.com
www.edcpub.com

Library of Congress Control Number: 2009931234

Printed and bound in the United States of America
1 2 3 4 5 6 7 8 9 10
ISBN: 978-1-935279-17-4

Dear Readers,

The story you're about to read is about me and my friends, and how we got mixed up in a case with Inspector Jacques. To save time, I'll introduce us all to you now. If you know us already, trot off to Chapter One.

I am Jack Russell, Dog Detective. I live with my landlord, Sarge, in Doggeroo. Sarge detects human-type crimes. I have the important job of detecting crimes that deal with dogs. I'm a Jack Russell terrier, so I am dogged and intelligent. Preacher lives with us. He is a clever, handsome junior Jack Russell. His mother is my friend Jill Russell.

Next door to Sarge and me live Auntie Tidge and Foxie. Auntie Tidge is lovely. She has biscuits, and fowls. Foxie is not lovely. He's a fox terrier (more or less). He used to be a street dog, and a thief, but he's reformed now. Auntie Tidge has even gotten rid of his fleas. Foxie sometimes helps me with my cases.

Uptown Lord Setter (Lord Red for short) lives in Uptown House with Caterina Smith. Lord Red means well, but he isn't very bright. Caterina and Sarge are going to get married.

Other friends and acquaintances in Doggeroo include Polly the dachshund, the Squekes, Ralf Boxer and Shuffle the pug. Then there's Fat Molly, but she's only the cat from the library.

That's all you need to know, so let's get on with Chapter One.

Yours doggedly,

Jack Russell — the detective with a nose for crime.

A Card From Caterina

Sarge was eating breakfast when the postman rattled the mailbox.

Preacher and I shot out our **dogdoor** to play the Postman Game, but we were too late. Preacher gave a little howl of disappointment as the postman rode on past Foxie's yard.

"That new postman doesn't play fair," said Foxie as he crawled under the hedge into our **terrier-tory**. "I don't like him." He sat down to scratch his ribs, then sniffed around to see if Preacher and I had left any breakfast in our bowls. Of paws, we hadn't.

Foxie grumbled about that. Then he left our yard (never mind how) and trotted off to visit Spotty Sprat. Spotty is a girl sprat from Polly Smote's last litter. She looks like Foxie, only littler and longer. She snaps at noses and tugs tails. Foxie loves her, but I **pre-fur** to keep my tail intact.

As Foxie disappeared, Sarge fetched the mail. "It's a card from Caterina," he said to

Preacher and me. "She says she's got a painter's pup for Uncle Smith. And that reminds me! We have to see if the **decorator** has finished Caterina's kitchen."

Caterina Smith and Lord Red were away at a dog show. They'd been gone for two weeks, and we all missed them.

"What's a painter's pup?" Preacher asked.

"It's a pup that lives with a painter, I **sup-paws**," I said. It didn't seem **im-paw-tant**, but it was.

<u>Jack's Facts</u>

Some things that seem im-paw-tant aren't.
Some things that don't seem im-paw-tant are.
It's hard to tell which is which until afterwards.
This is a fact.

The **terrier-phone** rang. Sarge grabbed the receiver and dropped the postcard on the hall table. "Hello, Kipps!"

Preacher waggled his tail. Inspector Kipper gave us treats at Sarge and Caterina's party. Preacher likes treats a bit too much. Terriers should be trim, slim and **terrier-ably** fast on their feet. Preacher is a bit **paw-tly**.

Jack's Facts

Good food is good.
Bad food is bad.
Too much good food leads to a paw-tly pup.
This is bad.
This is a fact.

"Caterina will be home soon," said Sarge. "In fact, I just had a card from her." He listened for a bit, then said, "Well, that sounds very mysterious, but it's no problem."

After a bit, Sarge hung up the terrier-phone. "Kipps says Inspector Cook from the Art Fraud Department wants to stay with us, boys," he told Preacher and me. "I expect we'll find out why when he arrives." He grinned. "I hope he likes dogs."

At lunchtime, we all went to Uptown House, to visit the decorator. It seemed strange to be in Red's **territory** and not see Red.

"What's a decorator?" asked Preacher.

"It's the person who came to paint Caterina's kitchen and look after the house while she's away," I said. "Caterina wanted the painting done while Lord Red wasn't here to put his paws in the paint."

Sarge knocked on the front door. After a while, the decorator opened it a little way. She had a floppy hat on, and she smelled

strongly of paint.

"Yes?" said the decorator.

"Caterina will be home soon, so I came to see how the work's going," said Sarge.

"It's fine, but you can't come in. You'll get paint on you." The decorator closed the door.

"Well!" said Sarge. He came back to Preacher and me, and we went home. I was glad to leave. The smell of paint disturbed my **super-sniffer**.

Jack's Glossary

Dogdoor. *A door especially for dogs.*

Terrier-tory. *A territory owned by a terrier.*

Pre-fur. *Prefer, for dogs.*

Decorator. *A person who decorates houses for other people.*

Sup-paws. *Suppose, for dogs.*

Im-paw-tant. *Important, for dogs.*

Terrier-phones. *Things that ring.*

Terrier-ably. *Very.*

Paw-tly. *Portly, or plump, for dogs.*

Territory. *A terrier-tory that belongs to a dog who is not a terrier.*

Super-sniffer. *Jack's nose in super-tracking mode.*

Invaders and Dog-Boggarts

Two days later I was home alone. Sarge was at work, Preacher had **disapawed** to visit Fat Molly at the library, and Foxie was at Polly's. I climbed in my basket, crawled under my special blanket, and prepared for a **Jack-nap**. Then our gate rattled.

I sniff-sniffed from under the blanket, and scented salami. I licked my chops, but then I smelled strangers: a person and a dog.

The gate clicked shut. Feet crunched and pattered up the steps. Keys jingled. The strange dog sniff-sniffed the air.

"Take care, Master, there is **un petit**

chien here," said the dog. He sounded funny.

"Quiet, Jacques," said the person. "Let's check the place before Russell gets home."

The door creaked. The strangers were invading our house! I leaped from my basket and **Jack-jumped** at the door with a volley of **Jack-yaps**. "Get off my terrier-tory!"

The dog was a black French bulldog with a jagged white patch on his chest. He stuck his tail in the air, hackled, and lifted one side of his lip to flash his fangs.

Snap! I had my **Jack-jaws** at his throat. A dog howled for mercy. That was me.

I backed away, chittering my teeth. The other dog smirked. I'd almost broken a fang on the metal studs of his collar!

As I set off to fetch Sarge, Auntie Tidge came out of her house with a plate of cake. I skidded to a stop.

"Oh, hello, **Jackie-wackie**," she said. "I hope you weren't growling at Inspector Cook. You must be teaching Preacher bad habits! Kitty Booker wants us to get him from the library. He's making some sort of fuss."

My junior Jack was in trouble! It must be

Fat Molly's fault.

Auntie Tidge walked up to our house and knocked on the door.

The invader opened it, and smiled. "Hello. You must be Miss Russell."

"Hello, Inspector Cook!" said Auntie Tidge. "My nephew telephoned to say he'd given you the house key. Welcome to Doggeroo!"

I licked my lips, and felt foolish. So, the invader was only Inspector Cook! I'd tried to chase Sarge's guest away, and I'd attacked his dog. This was not good.

I made a **snap decision**. Auntie Tidge could deal with Cook. I would rescue my junior Jack.

I left our yard (never mind how) and set off for the library.

As I approached, I made a **nose map**.

Jack's map:

1. *Kitty Booker.*

2. *Fat Molly.*

3. *Strange children.*

4. *Preacher.*

I had just finished my map when I heard squeals. Then came a yelp from Preacher. I knew it! Fat Molly had attacked the children *and* my junior Jack! I galloped to the rescue.

At the library, Preacher cowered against

the railing, whining with terror. Children bounced around. None of them seemed hurt, but where was Fat Molly? Then I realized Molly wasn't the problem. Preacher was afraid of the *children*! One of them dashed up and grabbed at him. "Doggy! Doggy!"

Preacher yelped and cried. The child laughed, and pounced again. "Doggy! Doggy!" It pulled Preacher's tail.

"Preacher, come to me!" I barked, but then I saw he was tied to the railing.

I barked and bounced so the child forgot Preacher and grabbed at me instead. The noise brought people from the library. One caught the child and Kitty Booker brought a rope and tied me next to Preacher. "Bad dogs!" she said.

Preacher whimpered, and showed the whites of his eyes. I gave him a quick

nose-over. He was terrier-ably upset.

"How did this happen?" I asked.

"I tried to teach Molly the Postman Game," said my junior Jack. "We were running across the road, when that postman almost hit us with his bike. Molly got away, but he tied me up. Then that **dog-boggart** grabbed me!"

<u>Jack's Facts</u>

Sometimes people think a dog is attacking when it is playing a game.
Sometimes dogs think humans are attacking when they're playing a game.
If dogs or humans are hurt or frightened by a game, it is a bad game.
This is a fact.

A child walked past. Preacher cringed again and tried to hide behind me. "I want to go home."

"Slip your collar," I said, but the postman had twisted the rope around the collar so it was too tight to slip. I lay down next to Preacher with my nose on my paws. "Go to sleep," I said. "I'll protect you."

I didn't mention the invaders. Preacher was miserable enough already.

Jack's Glossary

Disapawed. *Disappeared, for dogs.*

Jack-nap. *A well-earned sleep when the detecting is done.*

Un petit chien. *A little dog, in French.*

Jack-jump. *A very athletic spring done by a Jack Russell terrier.*

Jack-yap. *A loud, piercing yap made by a Jack Russell terrier.*

Jack-jaws. *The splendid set of jaws owned by a Jack Russell terrier.*

Jackie-wackie. *Auntie Tidge is the only person allowed to call me that.*

Snap decision. *A decision made quickly. Terriers are good at snapping, and at decisions.*

Nose map. *Way of storing information collected by the nose.*

Nose-over. *Health check carried out by the nose.*

Dog-boggarts. *Small, fast-moving children who grab dogs.*

 Rescued

Suddenly, my super-sniffer detected salami. I sat up. Preacher sniff-sniffed the air. "Someone's bringing us salami, Dad! Will he rescue me from the dog-boggarts?"

"*I* rescued you from the dog-boggarts," I pointed out. "The person with salami is Inspector Cook. He has a pawfully horrible dog called Jacques. Here they come."

Jacques sneered when he saw us, but Inspector Cook reached in his pocket and took out some salami. Preacher waggled his tail and licked his chops. In a second, my junior Jack swallowed the treat.

"Yummy salami!" he said, still waggling.

"Hello, **enfant**," said Jacques. He waved the tip of his tail.

Jack's Facts

Dogs wag their tails in different ways for different reasons.
Some wags are friendly. Some are not.
It pays to know the difference.
This is a fact.

Preacher rolled over to show his belly.

"Preacher, don't **submit**!" I ordered. "Doggeroo is our terrier-tory."

"Mademoiselle Russell told my master of your **paw-dicament**. We have come to your aid," said Jacques.

Preacher scrambled up. "Why do you talk funny?" he asked. "And what's Mademoiselle Russell?"

"I am Inspector Jacques. My first owners were French, so I speak as they do," said Jacques. "Mademoiselle Russell is the lady of the cake."

"You mean Auntie Tidge!" said Preacher. "Dad, Jacques is a friend. He knows Auntie Tidge!"

"**Bien**!" said Jacques. "Auntie Tidge! I put her in my **smell-bank**."

I lifted my lip. He was no friend of mine. I didn't want him to have Auntie Tidge in his smell-bank.

"We don't need your help. I already rescued Preacher," I snarled.

"And someone tied you by the neck to a post!" Jacques waved the tip of his tail again. "So we must rescue the rescuer."

I was about to tell him I could slip my collar when Inspector Cook untied me.

Preacher grinned up at him. "More salami?" he suggested. He seemed to have forgotten the dog-boggarts.

Inspector Cook dropped another piece into Preacher's waiting Jack-jaws. He offered some to me. It smelled good, but I turned my nose away.

Jack's Facts

Jacks are not greedy, but they do gulp food. A Jack that does not gulp food is either ill or

*pawfully **dog-stracted**.*

This is a fact.

As we walked home, the three Squekes crowded to their gate.

"Jack! Jack! Who's your friend?" they yaffled.

I would have said Jacques was no friend of mine, but he got in first.

"Greetings!" he said. "I am Inspector Jacques, a trained dog detective."

"A trained dog detective!" shrilled the Squekes. Their little beady eyes glittered under their hair.

Next, we passed Ralf Boxer, with his friend the Ruthless Rooster. "Jack Russell! Preacher! Who are your friends?" yapped Ralf.

Again, Jacques interrupted. "My master and I are detectives. We rescued Jack and Preacher, who were tied by the neck at the library."

Jill Russell called to us from across the road. "Jack! Preacher!"

"Mum Russell!" squealed Preacher. "This is Inspector Jacques and – "

"Wait!" Jill glanced up and down the road. She has **road sense**. If Preacher had more of that we wouldn't be in this mess now.

I wanted to explain things to Jill, but Inspector Cook tugged me back. "You dogs have caused enough trouble. I'm taking you home."

Jacques trotted across the road to Jill and sniffed noses with her. I hackled and lifted my lip. "Stay away from Jill Russell!" I snarled as Jacques returned.

"Bad dog!" said Cook. He dragged me away.

"Jill!" I yapped. "Wait!" But Jill trotted off towards the station.

Jack's Glossary

Enfant. *Child, in French.*

Submit. *Roll over to show another dog that you acknowledge its authority.*

Paw-dicament. *A predicament, for dogs. A difficult situation.*

Bien. *Good, in French.*

Smell-bank. *A store of smells that must be remembered.*

Dogstracted. *Distracted, for dogs.*

Road sense. *The sense to be careful when using the road.*

Locked Out

When we got home, Inspector Cook took Preacher and Jacques into the house. I tried to follow, but the dogdoor swung back and hurt my nose.

I banged it with my paws, then Jack-jumped back as the main door came open.

"Bad dog! Stay outside," growled Cook, pointing at me. He shut the door and locked the dogdoor on the inside.

I was barred from my own house! And Jacques was in there with my junior Jack. *Inspector* Jacques indeed! I was about to go and complain to Auntie Tidge when the dogdoor creaked and Jacques came out. I hackled.

"But no!" he said. "I have not come to fight, but to **paw-ley**." He stopped almost nose to nose with me.

I refused to back away. This was *my* terrier-tory. "What are you up to?" I growled.

"My master and I are here on a case," said Jacques. "Do you understand that?"

"Of paws I understand!" I said. "I'm Jack Russell, Dog Detective!"

Jacques laughed. "I outrank you."

"There's only one **top dog** in this terrier-tory," I snapped.

"I am your su-paw-rior! I live with an inspector. You live with a sergeant. I have a long pedigree and come from a noble breed. I am trained in detection. You have no pedigree, and perhaps no training. You observe my collar? It is my badge of office. It warns off criminals who seek to do me harm."

I **muttered**. I wasn't surprised criminals wanted to do Jacques harm. I might have wanted to harm him too, if my fangs had felt up to the job.

"I am not **interrier-ested** in your pedigree," I said. "My friend **Lord Setter of**

29

Uptown House has a pedigree longer than his tail, but he knows I'm top dog. Tell me about your case."

"It is most **paw-plexing**. It involves a painting of a dog which was stolen from the City Museum. My master believes that painting is here in Doggeroo. I, Jacques, am trained to track it down."

"Who cares about paintings of dogs?" I asked. "Proper dog detectives investigate cases that interest real dogs."

"You cannot see past your belly and your basket," said Jacques. He yapped and Cook let him back in. I tried to follow, but Cook put his boot in the way.

When Sarge came home, I **greeted** him with relief. Sarge let me in, of paws.

Inspector Cook sat at our table, drinking

from Sarge's mug and eating salami and cake from Auntie Tidge's plate. Jacques and Preacher watched.

"I see you've made yourself at home," said Sarge. "Why did you shut Jack out?"

"He attacked Jacques," said Cook.

"Jacques must have challenged him. Jack gets on well with other dogs, as long as they know their places." Sarge sat down. "What brings you to Doggeroo, Inspector Cook? Kipps didn't explain."

"I'm on the trail of the art thief and forger known as the Painter." Cook looked hard at Sarge.

Sarge laughed. "Never heard of him, but art crime is outside my area. What makes you think he's in Doggeroo?"

"A reliable source sent me a tip-off. What do you think of that, Sergeant Russell?"

"Art theft in Doggeroo? It doesn't make sense," said Sarge.

"The thefts were committed in many places. The latest, an important painting called *The Painter's Dog*, was stolen from the City Museum. Our tip-off suggests the Painter will bring it here, make copies and pass it on to a buyer."

"What kind of tip-off?" asked Sarge.

"My contact intercepted a coded postcard sent to a Doggeroo address." Cook stared at Sarge. He reminded me of Foxie **eyeing** Auntie Tidge's hens.

"Secret codes? Stolen paintings? In *Doggeroo*? It sounds like nonsense."

It sounded like nonsense to me, too. I decided I didn't like Cook, even if he did have salami. Visitors should know their places. Jacques and his master did not.

Jack's Glossary

Paw-ley. *Like parley, for dogs. Talking something over.*

Top dog. *The most important dog in a terrier-tory.*

Mutter. *A low rumble that is not quite a growl.*

Interrier-ested. *Interested, for terriers.*

Lord Setter of Uptown House. *Lord Red's pedigree name.*

Paw-plexing. *Strange and puzzling. Difficult for a dog to understand.*

Greet. *This is done by rising to the hind legs and clutching a person with the paws while slurping them up the face.*

Eyeing. *Staring hard at fowls or small furry creatures.*

Jacks On the Track

That night, Jacques left our yard (I'm not sure how).

Preacher yawned. "Where's Jacques going, Dad?"

"Let's find out," I said. "I don't trust him."

Preacher **pawsed**. "What if the dog-boggarts get me?"

I told him the dog-boggarts were asleep. We left the yard (never mind how) and followed Jacques. He was easy to track, because he smelled of salami. He trotted past Foxie's gate, and I heard a greedy sniff-sniffing from my pal.

"Is Jacques after Auntie Tidge's hens?" asked Preacher, but Jacques went to the Squekes' place, and yapped. "Attention!"

The Squekes yaffled to their gate. Their little eyes and sharp fangs gleamed in the moonlight. "Yes? Yes? Yes? What?"

"Have you smelled paint upon anyone lately, my friends?" asked Jacques.

The Squekes **con-furred**. "No. No. Not us," they yaffled.

Jacques went on, and Preacher and I followed. "Are you helping Inspector Jacques with his case, Jack?" asked the Squekes as we passed.

I **ig-gnawed** that.

Next, Jacques questioned Ralf Boxer, and then Jill Russell. I was pawfully fed up with Jacques and his questions. Who cared about paint? The only paint I knew about was what the decorator was using at Uptown House.

When Jacques had moved on, we talked to Jill. She poked me with her nose (she always does that), then gave Preacher a face wash. "You've been eating salami."

"Yummy," agreed Preacher.

Jill sniffed. "This Jacques acts like top dog

of Doggeroo. You should put him in his place, Jack." She poked me with her nose again, and trotted back to the station.

We followed Jacques past the river and up the hill. When we reached Uptown House, he sniff-sniffed around, then lifted his leg and did what dogs do.

"It's not **pawlite** to do that on Lord Red's territory," said Preacher.

Jacques sniff-sniffed his way along the fence until he came to a gap. He got down on his elbows and crawled into Red's yard.

"Is he stealing Red's toys?" asked Preacher.

"Yes, is he?" Foxie had caught up with us. "If there's a **canine criminal** in Doggeroo, I'll hide my boot." He sniffed hard, and began to drool. "I smell sausage. Has he stolen a sausage? Arrest him, Jack. I'll impound the sausage."

"In your belly, I sup-paws! But there's no sausage in this case," I said.

Foxie scratched his elbow. "There is sausage. I've been tracking it halfway around Doggeroo. If this bulldog has stolen it, arrest him."

"Jacques did not steal sausage," I said. "No one stole sausage. There is no sausage. What you smell is salami."

"Jacques's person has salami," said Preacher.

"Where? When? Who stole it? I want it!"

"Stop it," I said. "Foxie, there is no stolen sausage. We are tracking Jacques."

"Why?"

"I don't trust him, or his master," I said. "They've come to make trouble."

We **lay doggo** and kept **obbo**. Jacques was still **pawtrolling** the **pawrimeter** of Red's territory. We heard him sniff-sniffing. I sniffed too, and smelled paint.

Suddenly, Jacques came out. "So, here is **Monsieur le Scruff Chien du Caniveau**," he said. He sneefled. "I, Inspector Jacques, have solved this paw-plexing case for my master. I have found the Painter's lair."

Jack's Glossary

Pawsed. *Stopped to think with paw upraised.*

Con-fur. *Talk things over, done by furry dogs.*

Ig-gnaw. *Ignore, done by dogs.*

Pawlite. *Polite, for dogs.*

Canine criminal. *A bad dog.*

Impound. *Put something away safely where no one else can get at it.*

Lay doggo. *Kept quiet so as not to be detected.*

Obbo. *Observation. Close watch.*

Pawtrolling. *Patrolling, done by a dog.*

Pawrimeter. *The outside of a dog's territory.*

Monsieur le Scruff Chien du Caniveau. *Mr. Scruffy Gutter Dog, in French.*

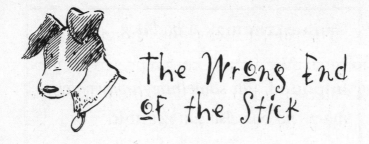

The Wrong End of the Stick

Foxie hackled. "What did you call me? And what's a painter? Is it the same as a decorator?"

"You are a scruffy gutter dog," said Jacques. "The Painter steals paintings of dogs, and makes copies. This house is the Painter's lair." He sneefled again. "The Painter uses paint. Here is the scent of paint. I detected this scent nowhere else in Doggeroo."

"This is Uptown House," I explained. "Caterina Smith and Lord Red live here. That smell is nothing to do with crime. Caterina Smith hired a decorator to paint her kitchen while she's away. That's what you smell."

"The Painter uses paint. Therefore, this house is the Painter's lair," repeated Jacques. "If Caterina Smith lives here, then she is the criminal we seek."

"Nonsense!" I snapped. "If Caterina was a criminal, Sarge would know."

"Sergeant Russell is the Painter's **accomplice**. His scent is here, cunningly masked by the smell of paint. He visits her in her lair," said Jacques. "This chain of evidence and deduction is obvious to the trained detective."

"You don't understand," said Preacher. "Caterina and Red have gone to a dog show. They're getting a painter's pup for Uncle Smith."

Jacques stiffened and his tail came up. "Exactly as my master suspected. The Painter will copy *The Painter's Dog* and sell it to this Uncle Smith."

I sighed. Jacques was as **obsessive** about criminals as Foxie was about sausages. "There are no paintings in this case," I insisted. "Caterina has a pup for Uncle Smith. Pups are not paintings. Pups are baby dogs."

Jacques slitted his eyes. "Do you take me for a fool? I know this *painter's pup* is a code, for my master says it is so. You try to make me believe it is a real dog."

"Of paws it's a real dog!" I said. "Why would Uncle Smith want a code dog?"

"He wouldn't," said Foxie. "He's got two real dogs already."

"Silence!" snarled Jacques. "You try to confuse me with talk of dogs! This *painter's pup* is a code name for *The Painter's Dog*, which the Painter stole from the City Museum."

"This is a silly case," said Foxie. "I'm hungry, and I'm going home."

Foxie scooted off and Preacher and I followed.

"Halt in the name of the paw!" snapped Jacques, but we ig-gnawed him.

Jack's Facts

Some dogs try to give orders to other dogs.

The best thing to do with this kind of order
is to ig-gnaw it.
This is a fact.

When we got home, Preacher crawled under our blanket and went to sleep. I kept obbo, in case of trouble.

Sure enough, it wasn't long before Jacques loomed over the basket.

"Back off," I growled. "This is *our* terrier-tory."

Jacques sat with his front paws together. "After you left, I investigated the Painter's van," he said. "I am sorry for you and **le petit** Preacher. The Painter is your friend, and your master is the Painter's accomplice."

I sighed. Jack Russell's the name, detection's the game, but my cases are always about dogs. This case was about people. It was not a suitable case for a dog detective.

"My master must **interrogate** Sergeant Russell, Caterina Smith and Uncle Smith," continued Jacques. "When they go to **prison**, you and Preacher will need a new home. Pawhaps my master will adopt you." He pawsed. "Then we shall see who is top dog, **non**?"

I bared my teeth. If Jacques thought I would submit to him, he had got hold of the wrong end of the stick.

Jack's Facts

Sometimes, people or dogs get hold of the wrong end of a stick.
It is usually easy for a dog to tell the right end.
The right end might be the end that makes sense.
Or it might be the end that has a sausage on it.
This is a fact.

Jack's Glossary

Accomplice. *Someone who helps a criminal do bad things.*

Obsessive. *Too interested in something.*

Le petit. *The little, in French.*

Interrogate. *Official questioning, done by someone who is not a terrier.*

Prison. *Like a pound, but for human criminals.*

Non. *No, in French.*

Dog-Boggarts Again

I had problems. Jacques and Cook thought my favorite people were criminals. Jill thought Jacques wanted to be top dog in Doggeroo. Preacher thought dog-boggarts were out to get him. How could I explain the situation to Sarge?

Jack's Facts

Some people are good at understanding **Dogspeak.**
It's easy for Sarge to understand "I'm hungry" or "back off."

It's not easy for him to understand "This person and his dog have the wrong end of the stick" or "Preacher is afraid of dog-boggarts because one grabbed him when he was tied up."
This is a fact.

At breakfast, I pointed at Cook and muttered. Sarge **nudged** me with his toe. "Stop that, Jack."

Preacher came in and waggled up to Cook. "Salami?" he said.

Cook gave him a piece. Preacher gulped it down. Cook offered some to me, but I turned my head away.

The postman rattled the mailbox, but I didn't play the Postman Game. Sarge started towards the door, and Cook followed him. When they came back, Sarge looked cross.

"What is going on?" he said to Cook. "Why did the postman give you *my* mail?"

"You tell me," said Cook.

"You have no right to pry into my mail."

Cook didn't answer. He just eyed Sarge again.

"What did you expect to find?" asked Sarge. "Anyone would think you were investigating *me*." He laughed.

Cook did not laugh. "I expect another coded message from the Painter. Like this one." He pulled a postcard out of his pocket. It was the one Caterina had sent Sarge. "You cannot deny this is yours," said Cook. "It was on your hall table when I arrived. It has your name on it."

Sarge stared. "Why would I deny it?"

"Because it is evidence against you," said Cook. "My brother is now the postman in

Doggeroo. He saw this coded card and recognized a clue to my case. He called me immediately."

"Don't be silly," said Sarge. "It's a postcard from Caterina. She's – "

"I intend to interview this Caterina, *and* her uncle," interrupted Cook. "This *painter's pup* is a reference to *The Painter's Dog*, the painting stolen from the City Museum."

Sarge pulled his postcard out of Cook's hand. "Caterina and her uncle do not steal paintings. Neither they nor I have anything to do with your case. You, and your brother, are wrong. You should look for *real* clues. Now, out of my way. I have an appointment, and then I have to meet a train."

Sarge took my leash from behind the door. "Coming, Jack?"

I wanted to go, but I decided to keep

obbo. Sarge took Preacher instead.

As soon as Sarge left, Cook and Jacques went to annoy Auntie Tidge. Of paws, I followed. Foxie was at home, eyeing the hens. He was not pleased to see Jacques.

"What does he want?" he asked me.

"Trouble," I said. It was the only thing I was sure of. "And his master wants to make trouble for Sarge and Caterina."

Foxie scratched his ear. "I'm off, before he makes trouble for *me*," he said. He left his yard (never mind how), and I went through Foxie's dogdoor. I found Jacques sniffing around the kitchen, poking his nose into Foxie's things.

"Stop that," I said.

"I am sniffing for clues," said Jacques.

"You won't find a clue in Foxie's old boot," I said.

Cook was questioning Auntie Tidge. "My brother tells me Caterina Smith will soon be back. Does she plan to bring the painting with her?"

"She's at a dog show. It's nothing to do with paintings," said Auntie Tidge.

"When will her uncle take delivery of the painting?"

Auntie Tidge frowned. "Uncle Smith is a farmer out near Jeandabah. He has nothing to do with paintings either."

"So, if I were to visit Caterina Smith's house, I would find no paintings of dogs?"

"She has one or two, I think. What's all this about, Inspector Cook?"

"Miss Russell, you must take me to Caterina Smith's house and show me these paintings. Right now."

Inspector Cook was bullying Auntie

Tidge! I eyed his leg, but I knew if I attacked him, Jacques might attack *me*. I had to get Sarge at once!

I shot out of Foxie's dogdoor.

"Stop, in the name of the paw!" barked Jacques, but I ig-gnawed him. The dogdoor shot back and clipped him on the nose.

My super-sniffer detected Sarge's tracks and Preacher's. I was following the trail when I heard Foxie barking. "Jack! Jack!"

I pawsed. Foxie might be in trouble! On the other paw, Auntie Tidge *was* in trouble. But Foxie was still barking. "Preacher needs you!"

Of paws, I set off at a gallop. I love Auntie Tidge, and Foxie is my pal, but Preacher is my junior Jack.

I met Foxie near the library. "Dog-boggarts," he panted. "Preacher is in trouble!"

Nose to the ground, I tracked Sarge and
Preacher to the school, where Preacher was
tied to the fence, whimpering with terror.
Sarge had gone in to give a talk to the
children, but five dog-boggarts had gathered
around my junior Jack. One was scolding
Preacher. "Bad dog! Bad dog!"

"Preacher!" I dove into the school yard,
scattering dog-boggarts. "What did you do to
that dog-boggart?"

"I only muttered to make them go away,"

he whined. He was so scared he'd made a puddle around his paws.

I barked at the children. They scattered again, but they didn't go far. Once more, I made a snap decision. "Preacher, slip your collar," I ordered. "Lift your nose, flatten your ears and *pull*."

Preacher obeyed. The collar slipped over his head and dropped on the ground. Preacher slunk after me as I scooted out of the school yard to join Foxie.

Jack's Glossary

Dogspeak. *The private language of dogs.*

Nudge. *A push that is not quite a kick.*

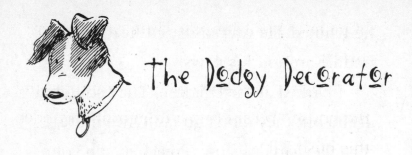

The Dodgy Decorator

Poor Preacher! His tail was low and he showed the whites of his eyes. I needed to dog-stract him from his fright, quickly.

"Preacher," I said, as we reached our street, "Cook took Auntie Tidge away. Use your super-sniffer to find out where."

Preacher sniff-sniffed at the footpath. Slowly, his tail came up, and he **pointed**.

"They got in Auntie Tidge's car. The scent goes towards Lord Red's territory."

We ran to Uptown House.

When we arrived, Auntie Tidge's car was parked behind the decorator's van. The smell of paint made it **im-paw-sible** to tell where anyone was.

"They're here somewhere," I said, circling the house. "Let's set up a **doggo obbo** under this bush. I'll – "

My instructions stopped there, because Jacques turned up.

"What have you done to Auntie Tidge?" yapped Foxie.

Jacques curled his lip. "Nothing, Monsieur le Scruff. I wish to paw-ley."

Foxie snarled.

"Don't," I said. "He has an anti-fang collar around his neck."

"He hasn't got one around his hind leg," said Foxie, and lunged.

Jacques yelped.

My junior Jack cringed, so I led him away from the snapping and snarling. We found Cook and Auntie Tidge by the front door.

"No one's home," Auntie Tidge said, "and I don't have a key."

"We'll see about that." Cook knocked on the door with his fist. Nothing happened. He knocked again. "The van is here, which means Caterina Smith is back and lying low."

"That's not Caterina's van. It belongs to the decorator." Auntie Tidge tapped her toe. "I *told* you. No one is home."

Cook thumped the door again.

"I'm going," said Auntie Tidge. "I'll tell my nephew about this."

As she bustled to her car, my ears picked up a stealthy sound inside the house.

"That decorator *is* here, and she's being dodgy," I told Preacher. I went to sniff-sniff the van, but the pong of paint overpowered any clues. I sneefled and sneezed. "We need Sarge," I said. "Jack Russell's the name, detection's the game, but it takes a human to deal with dodgy decorators and obsessed inspectors."

Preacher whimpered. "Sarge is where the dog-boggarts are."

It was time for another snap decision. "I'll go for Sarge," I said. "You go to wait for the train. If Caterina and Red arrive, stay with them."

I took Preacher to the station, then went to the school. I dodged dog-boggarts and teachers until I found Sarge. I scooted up and launched a **Jack-attack** at his trouser leg.

"Stop that, Jack!" said Sarge.

The children laughed and squealed and tried to grab me.

"No!" said Sarge sternly. "Grabbing dogs

scares them. They might bite in self-defense."

"The little fat dog was scared, but he didn't bite. He just ran away," said one of the dog-boggarts who had upset Preacher.

Sarge picked me up and told the children to stay inside. He carried me to where he had left Preacher, and stared at the empty collar. "Jack? Where's Preacher?"

I knew, of paws, but before I could show Sarge, Auntie Tidge drove up. She wound down her car window.

"Dear, that Inspector Cook is being silly. He made me take him to Caterina's place to look for pictures of dogs. He thinks we're *criminals*."

"Cook thinks too many things," said Sarge. "Where is he now?"

"He's at Uptown House, trying to bully the decorator. He thinks she's Caterina. I don't think she's home," said Auntie Tidge.

Sarge looked at his watch. "I have to be at the station to meet Caterina's train, but I'll go to Uptown House first. You go on home, Auntie. If you see Preacher, look after him until I come back." He snapped his fingers to me. "Come on, Jack."

When we reached Uptown House, Cook was trying to open the decorator's van. I couldn't see Jacques, but I heard yapping behind the house. I trotted around to investigate.

Foxie and Jacques were on their hind legs, sniff-sniffing at the open window. On the other side, the decorator made shooing motions with her hands. So she *was* there.

"Biscuits," said Foxie. "Mine! Mine!"

Jacques licked his lips. "Greetings, my friend."

"I'm not your friend," I said, hackling. "And you're not mine."

The decorator tossed out a biscuit. Foxie caught it. "More!" he yapped.

"Sshhhhh!" The decorator threw another biscuit. It landed in the flower bed. Foxie dove for it.

Jacques said, "That decorator bribes us to be quiet." He chuckled, as Foxie yapped again. "It does not work with Monsieur le Scruff."

"Feeding Foxie makes him louder," I agreed. "What is she doing?"

I thought Jacques would ig-gnaw me, but he said, "I believe the decorator wants to escape through the window, to avoid our masters."

"That makes sense," I agreed. It was about the only thing that did.

We looked up at the decorator. She had a

bucket of water. We backed away.

"She acts suspiciously," said Jacques as water splashed the ground where we had been. "If not for the evidence of the painter's pup, which accuses Caterina Smith and your master, I would suspect this decorator of the crime."

"Listen!" I said. "The painter's pup has *nothing* to do with the situation. You might be a trained detective, but you don't know everything."

"What could a common dog such as you know that I do not?" sneered Jacques.

"I know Caterina Smith. I know Sarge. I know Uncle Smith. They are interested in real pups. They are *not* interested in paintings. It's like knowing Foxie. I know he would steal sausage, or cake. He would *not* steal a banana."

I thought Jacques would sneer again, but he sneefled thoughtfully. "So! You have **local knowledge**, my friend," he said. "I had not taken that into account, and neither did my master. I was mistaken about you. You are indeed a proper dog detective." He dodged as the decorator flung another bucket of water at us.

"Biscuits! Biscuits! Mine! Mine!" yapped Foxie. He had a mad gleam in his eyes.

"But about Monsieur le Scruff I am not mistaken," added Jacques. "Come, let us see what our masters are doing. Monsieur le Scruff will keep this suspect busy."

We found Cook and Sarge arguing by the van.

"I don't have time for this," snapped Sarge. "I have to meet Caterina's train."

"To warn her to dispose of the evidence?"

"No, to warn her about your strange obsession. If you want to get in that van, ask the owner." Sarge marched over to the house. "That decorator can't have slipped out the back. This is the only door," he said. "Police! Open up!"

There was no back door, but there *was* a window. I shot into action. First, I Jack-attacked

Sarge's trousers. Then I barked. Jacques followed my example. I Jack-attacked again, then we rushed around the house, where Foxie joined us in a **pan-dog-monium**.

Jack's Glossary

Pointed. *Clever dogs use their noses to point to things.*

Im-paw-sible. *Impossible, for dogs.*

Doggo obbo. *Official observation, performed by a dog.*

Jack-attack. *Growling and biting and worrying at trouser legs. Very loud, quite harmless.*

Local knowledge. *Things dogs know because of who and where they are.*

Pan-dog-monium. *A lot of noise that involves dogs.*

The Painter's Pup

The dodgy decorator was halfway out the window. When she heard the pan-dog-monium, she slithered the rest of the way and ran for the van.

She might have got away if she hadn't stubbed her toe on Foxie. Over she went, nearly squashing Jacques and me.

"Biscuits!" yelled Foxie, and stuck his nose in her pocket.

The pan-dog-monium continued until Sarge and Cook dashed up.

"Quiet, Jacques!" said Cook.

"Jack! Foxie! That's enough!" yelled Sarge.

Jacques and I stopped, but Foxie yapped

on about biscuits.

"Are you all right?" Sarge asked the dodgy decorator, helping her up.

She glared at us. "Your dogs attacked me while I was getting out the window."

"Why the window?" asked Sarge. "What's wrong with the door?"

The decorator stared at her toes.

"What do you know about *The Painter's Dog*?" asked Cook.

"I'm leaving," said the decorator. "I won't stay in a place where people bang on doors and dogs fight under windows. I'm leaving in my van. Right now." She marched past Cook and Sarge.

We followed. The decorator looked worried. "I'm going," she said again. "There's no law against climbing out of windows."

"You're right," said Sarge. "Goodbye."

"Now you just wait a minute!" said Cook.

The decorator took a key out of her
pocket and unlocked the front of the vehicle.
She put one foot on the step ... then
staggered backwards as Jacques sprang past
her. He slithered over the seat and into the
back of the van.

We heard him sneefling and sneezing,
then he barked, "Master! Master! Master!"

In seconds, Foxie hopped in too, still
yelling about biscuits.

"Get those dogs out of there!" snapped

the decorator. "They'll *ruin* the paintings!"
Then she dropped the keys and clapped her
hand over her mouth.

Sarge picked up the keys and unlocked
the back of the van. It was full of Jacques,
Foxie ... and paintings of dogs.

"I think this is all the evidence you
need," said Sarge.

Cook pulled out a painting. "*The
Painter's Dog* from the City Museum!" he
said. "And I see several copies. The game's
up, Painter." He turned to Sarge. "Sergeant
Russell, I'm arresting this person for the
theft and forgery of *The Painter's Dog* and
several other artworks. Arrange for
immediate transfer of the prisoner to – "

He went on and on, but Sarge and I
stopped listening. A distant whistle told us
the train from the city had arrived at
Doggeroo Station.

"Time to go," said Sarge. "Foxie! Out of that van!"

"Sergeant, secure the evidence," said Cook. "These are valuable artworks."

Sarge shook his head. "*You* secure the evidence. It's your case. I have to go to the station to meet Caterina." He grinned at Cook. "She won't be very pleased to hear she employed an art thief instead of a decorator to paint her kitchen."

"Oi!" said the decorator. "I *am* a decorator. I just like paintings of dogs." She gave me a nasty look. "Though after this I wish I'd taken cat pictures instead."

Sarge, Foxie and I set off down the hill. We'd almost reached Doggeroo Station when Jacques caught up.

"I wish to see for myself this Caterina Smith and this painter's pup," said Jacques.

I made a nose map.

Jack's map:

1. Train smells.

2. Jill Russell.

3. Preacher.

4. Caterina Smith.

5. Lord Red.

6. Strange pup.

"Then come this way!" I yapped, and shot off ahead of Sarge to the platform where Caterina and Red had just left the train. Of paws, Jill Russell and Preacher were there to greet them.

"There you are, Preacher!" said Sarge. He hugged Caterina. Caterina hugged Preacher and me. Preacher squealed with excitement.

Lord Red bounded along the platform. "Jack! Jack! Did you miss me? Jack, I won a new ribbon. I was Champion Dog again. Preacher, did you miss me?" His tail went around and around, and his ears bounced.

"Lordie! Lordeeeeee!" called Caterina. Red galloped away.

"Where is this painter's pup?" asked Jacques.

I pawsed. Where *was* the painter's pup?

Then I saw Caterina had a pet carrier. She opened it, and out waddled a small dog. He was the same colour as Red, but he had big sploshes of white on him.

"Meet Uncle Smith's new pup," said

Caterina. "He's a painted setter, and very rare. His father is called Painter's Pride."

Sarge laughed. "So *that's* the painter's pup! You can't imagine how much trouble he's caused."

"Mafff!" said the painter's pup, swirling his little tail.

"What trouble?" asked Caterina. "And who's the bulldog?"

"He belongs to Inspector Cook, who is at your place, arresting your decorator."

Caterina stared. "Whatever for?"

Sarge laughed. "It's a long story."

I sup-paws Sarge explained everything to Caterina, but Lord Red galloped up and nearly knocked me over, so I didn't hear any more.

"So," said Jacques, as we all left the station, "your local knowledge proved better than my special training, non?"

I remembered how Jacques had sprung into the back of the Painter's van to detect the paintings.

"They both came in useful," I said.

"Pawhaps we might work together again, my friend?"

But I thought I'd stick to the kinds of cases that interest a *proper* dog detective, and leave things like stolen paintings to Inspector Jacques.

About the Authors

Darrel and Sally Odgers live in Tasmania with their Jack Russell terriers, Tess, Trump, Pipwen, Jeanie and Preacher, who compete to take them for walks. They enjoy walks, because that's when they plan their stories. They toss ideas around and pick the best. They are also the authors of the popular *Pet Vet* series.

PET VET The new series from the authors of Jack Russell: Dog Detective!

Meet Trump! She's an A.L.O., or Animal Liaison Officer. She works with Dr. Jeanie, the young vet who runs Pet Vet Clinic in the country town of Cowfork. Dr. Jeanie looks after animals that are sick or injured. She also explains things to the owners. But what about the animals? Who will tell them what's going on? That's where Trump comes in.

JACK RUSSELL:
Dog Detective

Read all of Jack's adventures!

Jack Russell:
the detective with
a nose for crime.